FINDING Us

A Music Within Short Story

By Faith Gibson

All words and Lyrics Copyright © 2018 by Faith Gibson
Published by: Bramblerose Press LLC
Editor: Jagged Rose Wordsmithing
First edition: December 2018
Print edition: April 2025
Print cover design: Faith Gibson
Cover photography: Deposit Photos, Adobe Stock
ISBN: 979-8991426169

Chapter One

"THIS IS IT, huh? Our last show together," Sloane said as he fell in step with Taggart Lee, lead singer for 7's Mistress. Emotions were high all the way around, what with Taggart Lee having just given notice he was quitting the band. The four of them had rocked the world for over fifteen years, so getting ready to step on the stage for the last time had Sloane's throat tight and his eyes misty. "I just want to tell you it's been an absolute honor to rock the stages with you, Lee," Sloane said, using the name only Tag's family called him. "You aren't just the best lead singer I've ever heard, but one of the best friends a guy could have. If Pauly and I decide to carry on, we want you to be our producer."

Pauly, guitarist as well as Sloane's best friend and lover, stopped them and pulled them both into a hug. The three of them stood quietly, enjoying their moment. Cade was still back in the conference room talking things over with the CEO of MG Records. Echo's high heels clicked across the concrete as she headed their way.

"Is this a private party or can anyone join?" their manager asked. Pauly stepped back and allowed Echo into their circle.

"I love you guys," she whispered before wiping at her tears.

"There's no crying in rock 'n' roll," Sloane teased.

"There sure as hell is," Tag responded. "I have a feeling tonight's going to be full of tears. This is the end of an era. And I want to say thank you, all of you, for having my back out there. And I'm sorry if you feel like I'm letting you down by going off in a different direction."

Pauly stepped next to Sloane and wrapped him up in his arms, kissing him in front of Tag and Echo. "I think it's safe to say we're ready to go in a different direction, too. What about you, Sunshine?" Pauly asked Echo when he broke the kiss. It wasn't the first time Pauly had been overly friendly with Sloane in front of the others. Having been bandmates and best friends for fifteen years, they were often touch feely around the others, but it was the first time they'd given any indication their relationship was more than that of friends. Maybe tonight was about lasts, but Sloane had hope it was also a night of firsts.

Echo smiled at all of them. "I'm willing to manage a really hot super couple if I ever find one," she said with a wink. "Erik and Bethany are center stage. Good luck out there, all of you. Let's go rock this bitch."

"You ready, Slick?" Pauly asked, using his nickname for Sloane. Sloane only nodded when he caught the mist in Pauly's gaze. If he spoke, he was afraid he'd be the one crying. When they reached center stage, the two men placed their

2

backs against each other. Normally, before the lights came all the way up, they moved apart and were on their respective sides of the stage. This time – the last time they would play together as 7's Mistress – Pauly remained where he was, strumming the opening notes to "Heaven's Hell." Their heads were leaned back against the other's shoulder, eyes closed, completely in sync. It wasn't until Tag greeted the crowd that they finally moved apart. Sloane wondered if that was Pauly's way of claiming him in front of the world. Then again, it was such a small gesture, he could be mistaken.

The show was more energetic than Sloane could remember. The band – even Cade – gave it their all, and the crowd fed off their energy. When Tag took the stage alone to sing his song for Erik, Sloane and Pauly stood off to the side, sharing a bottle of water. Sloane wanted that. He wanted what Tag had found with his pediatrician boyfriend – the kind of love worthy of songs. Worth leaving your band for. Worth telling your man in front of twenty thousand fans you wanted forever with them. He glanced over at Pauly who was already looking at him. He didn't know who leaned in first, but their lips met in a kiss so sweet, Sloane's heart skipped a beat.

When the crowd roared, they broke apart and returned to their places on stage. Tag was being helped back onto the platform by security guards. The grin he gave them was bright enough to power the arena. Yeah, Sloane wanted that, and he wanted it with Pauly.

3

The high from the night turned pretty damn low when Erik's friend Sarah held the babysitter at gunpoint with both Delilah and Brady, Bethany's baby boy, in the house as hostages. The ending was tragic, with Sarah taking her own life. The good news was everyone else, including both kids, weren't harmed.

For Tag and Erik, things settled down, and the two of them recovered from the scare with their love stronger. For Sloane and Pauly, things stalled out. Instead of spending the two weeks before Christmas alone, Pauly wanted to hang out with the others so he could play with Delilah. Sloane wasn't jealous. Not really, but he had thought their lives would progress together. Granted, it had only been two weeks since their last show, so maybe Pauly was trying to figure out what his new normal would be.

Watching his lover snuggle the baby was bittersweet. Pauly was a natural with Delilah, and Sloane had to wonder how his man would be with his own kids. Both had lived rock star lives early on, bedding both men and women. Sloane had even married the mother of his daughter, however short-lived it was. Being on the road eleven months out of the year was no way to be a husband or father. Sloane talked to his daughter, Taryn, at least once a month, but he hadn't seen her in over a year. As far as Sloane knew, Pauly hadn't seen his kids in almost five years. Watching Tag raise Delilah added to the guilt Sloane dealt with every day.

4

Tag had decided to leave 7's Mistress to be more hands-on in raising Delilah with Erik, leaving Sloane, Pauly, and Cade at a crossroads. With Cade at odds with the rest of the band, that left Sloane and Pauly to figure out what was next for the two of them. Over the last few years, they had gone from sharing lovers after shows to reaching only for each other when it came time to scratch their itch. They had been best friends for almost fifteen years, and having their relationship move toward intimate had been as natural as breathing.

"Merry Christmas." Tag stood behind Sloane, looking over his shoulder at the crowd in the living room. It didn't matter that the band had officially broken up; all of them, save Cade, were gathered in Tag and Erik's home to celebrate the holidays. Two of their security detail were hanging out as well, talking of starting their own company there in Nashville so they could stay close to Delilah. One little baby had managed to turn the music world on its ear when she lost her momma, and her world-famous rock star uncle gained custody.

"It's a beautiful thing you got here," Sloane said in response, and he meant it. This same time last year, the band was in Japan, rocking to a sold-out stadium. Tag did his best to get home to his sister every year for Christmas since it was just the two of them. Cade had his folks in California, and Sloane and Pauly usually wound up back in LA drinking until New Years was over. Being with Tag and his new family was

5

so out of character for all of them, but it was something Sloane would have to get used to if he wanted to keep Pauly in his life.

Sloane tracked Pauly as he handed the baby off to Erik and left the room. *Speaking of beautiful.* Sloane's feelings for his best friend had turned from platonic to falling-off-the-edge-of-a-cliff, in-your-face, head-over-heels, every-cliché-under-the-sun, love. Pauly didn't speak of his feelings, but Sloane felt loved every time his lover turned those stormy gray eyes his way. Every time he brushed against Sloane, lingering a bit longer than friends should. Every time he subconsciously pulled him closer in the middle of the night.

They hadn't talked about what they were going to do now that 7's Mistress was no more. They hadn't talked about much of anything. Tag, who was looking to start his own production company, said he was okay with the remaining members forming their own band, but with Cade in the wind, Sloane knew that wouldn't happen. He wasn't sure he wanted it to happen. The four of them had played hard-driving rock for as long as they'd been together, and Sloane was ready to slow things down a bit. It wasn't like he needed the money. Even sending his ex-wife and daughter a monthly check didn't put a dent in his bank account. Now was the time to do something different.

"Have you figured out your next steps?" Tag asked.

"Watching you and Erik… It makes me wish for my own

6

family." Sloane was ready for a new normal. He wanted to do everyday things like shopping for groceries, cooking dinner before vegging out on the sofa watching inane shows on Netflix. He wanted to go see a movie on the weekends. Get a dog like Duke he could take on walks and play fetch with. And he wanted all that with Pauly.

"You mean with Tracy and Taryn?"

Sloane never considered trying to get his ex and daughter back. Even if he had, it didn't matter. She'd moved on and had remarried. Sloane just never talked about them to the rest of the band. Not even Pauly. Some things were best left in the past. Before he could answer, Pauly shouldered past and said, "I'm headed to the hotel." He didn't wait to see if Sloane was ready to go.

"Hold up," Sloane said, but Pauly shook his head.

"I'll catch up with you later." Pauly said his goodbyes to everyone except Sloane, and didn't that feel like a punch to the gut. Sloane didn't let the others see how his best friend's abrupt departure hurt his feelings. They had spent every available moment together for a long time, and maybe Pauly just needed some space. Sloane would give it to him. For a little while.

Tag picked back up on the conversation they had been having. "Are you seriously thinking of going back to Tracy?"

"What? Hell no. My life is with Pauly. At least I hope it is. Besides, Tracy's remarried. Taryn likes the guy, says he

7

treats them both well. That's all I can hope for where the two of them are concerned. Now that I'm not on the road eleven months out of the year, I do want to spend more time with Taryn. Get to know my daughter before she's completely grown."

Tag squeezed Sloane's shoulder. "I'm sure you and Pauly will be fine. You know how he gets."

"Everything okay?" Erik asked when he joined the two of them.

Sloane didn't know how to answer, so he shrugged. "Today was emotional for all of us." After passing out gifts, Tag and Erik both asking the other to marry him, and visiting the cemetery where Tag's sister was buried, the day had been filled with both tears and laughter, so Sloane could see why Pauly would want some alone time. Considering they were sharing a hotel room, that meant he had to find somewhere else to go to give Pauly his space.

Tag looked like he wanted to say something, but Sloane waved him off. "I'm just gonna go look at some lights. I'll probably see you tomorrow." He made the rounds, wishing everyone a Merry Christmas, and walked out the front door, pulling on his coat. Pauly must have called for a ride since the rental was still in the driveway. Sloane slid into the driver's seat and headed away from the small community where Erik's house was. He did what he told Tag and just drove around for hours, thinking about the future.

By the time he entered the hotel room in downtown Nashville, his heart was heavy. Pauly was already asleep. Sloane considered sleeping in the second bedroom of their suite, but he didn't want to be alone. After stripping down to his briefs, he climbed in bed behind Pauly and pulled his best friend close. Pauly snuggled back into Sloane as he always did, and only then was Sloane able to let go of some of the stress.

During the hours spent riding around, Sloane decided he needed to get away from Tag and Erik. Away from the blissfulness that he wanted for himself. He didn't know if Pauly would go with him, but if he didn't want to, Sloane would be okay. He had to be. After worrying about the future for what felt like hours, Sloane's eyes finally drifted closed.

Standing at the bathroom counter, Sloane admitted to Pauly's reflection in the mirror, "I can't stay here."

"Here as in the hotel, or here as in Nashville?"

"Nashville. Don't get me wrong. I'm happy for Tag and Erik, and I love Delilah, but… I'm kind of… lost."

"Then let's go find you," Pauly said, wrapping his arms around Sloane's waist, resting his chin on Sloane's shoulder.

Sloane sighed. He should've known Pauly would understand. Turning in his lover's arms, Sloane ran his hands through Pauly's long hair, tilting his head back to have access to the long stretch of skin that was Pauly's throat. Sloane loved nipping at Pauly's Adam's apple, licking a path across his jaw

9

to his ear lobe, where he bit down hard enough to make Pauly gasp. Pauly slid his hands down Sloane's back until he was gripping Sloane's ass. Grinding their hard-ons together, Pauly muttered, "Bed." Sloane didn't hesitate to follow when Pauly grabbed his hand, leading him from the bathroom. Pauly pushed Sloane onto his back before crawling between Sloane's legs and pulled his briefs down his thighs just far enough he could suck on his hard cock. Pauly didn't bother edging Sloane. He took Sloane's dick all the way down, using his hand to add extra friction.

Sloane gripped Pauly's hair, pulling and pushing. He wanted to come, but he wanted to do it while Pauly was balls deep in his ass. "No," he husked. "Not yet." Pauly pulled off without preamble and ripped Sloane's briefs down his legs, tossing them to the floor. He grasped Sloane's legs, pushing them back to his chest. With no lube and no hesitation, Pauly shoved his hard length into Sloane. The burn was painful, but it let him know he was alive. Pauly didn't last long, just a few thrusts and he said, "Grab your dick." Sloane knew his lover was close, but so was he, primed from the blowjob. When Sloane's orgasm hit, his ass bore down on Pauly's cock, and his lover was coming with him. Pauly pulled out and rolled to his side. Sloane couldn't be bothered to get up and clean himself. No, he wanted Pauly's cum to stay with him as long as possible. He rolled onto Pauly's chest and nestled his face in his friend's neck, sleep taking him quickly.

Chapter Two

WHEN SLOANE WOKE, he stretched his arm across the bed, reaching for Pauly. The smile he still wore fell when he found the spot was empty, and the sheets were cold. Fuck, it had just been a dream. Rolling onto his back, Sloane remembered how things had ended the day before. He listened for movement from the other room, praying Pauly hadn't walked out. When the sound of a guitar being strummed met his ears, he let out the breath he'd been holding. Sloane rolled out of bed, took care of business in the bathroom, and padded barefoot into the living area of the suite.

Pauly either didn't hear him or was lost in the melody he was playing. It wasn't a song Sloane had heard, so Pauly was more than likely creating what could become a new hit record. Only instead of it being hard and heavy, the tune was slower. Lyrics immediately began to take hold in Sloane's mind. Standing behind the sofa, Sloane carded his fingers through Pauly's long hair.

Pauly stopped playing, but he didn't speak. "You okay?" Sloane asked.

"Why wouldn't I be?" Pauly stood abruptly, Sloane's

fingers falling away. Pauly set his guitar on the sofa, standing in place as if he was waiting for something.

Sloane took a good look at his best friend. Pauly's shoulders were slumped, and he ran a hand through his long hair. Something was definitely bothering Pauly, but he wasn't one to open up about his feelings. Instead of continuing that line of questioning, Sloane asked, "What are we going to do?"

"About?" Pauly asked as he moved into the kitchen, pouring the last cup of coffee. Damn, he'd been up awhile.

"The future." Sloane didn't add 'of our music' because he felt that was a given.

"I think you already have things figured out, so why don't you tell me?" Pauly kept his back to Sloane, and Sloane couldn't figure out what had happened between the time they woke happily yesterday to last night.

"I don't, that's why I'm asking."

"You want a family, and I want to stay here, make music, and help out with Delilah," Pauly snapped, finally turning to look at Sloane.

Sloane was taken aback at Pauly's tone. Yes, he wanted a family, but he wanted that with Pauly. He'd hoped his lover wanted the same thing, but apparently not.

"I had hoped we could spend New Year's together."

"And we can't do that here?"

"We can, but I really need to get away for a while," Sloane admitted. He loved his music family, but they'd all been together every day for the last couple weeks. He wanted alone time with Pauly.

"And I need to stay here."

Sloane hesitated before he said, "Then I guess I'll hit the road." *Please say you'll come with me. Please ask me not to go.*

Pauly shrugged, and that hurt as much or more than his lack of words. Defeated, Sloane went back to his – their – room to pack. He didn't have a lot of clothes there. All their things from the road had been packed up and shipped back to their homes in LA. Sloane didn't see himself staying in California alone, but he needed... Hell, he didn't know what he needed. Maybe giving Pauly some space would give him time to figure out what his next steps were. Sloane needed to do the same, especially if he was going to have to go solo.

By the time he had his duffel packed, Pauly was standing in the door, leaning against the frame. Sloane stopped in front of Pauly, hiking the strap of his bag onto his shoulder. "Sure you don't want to come with me?" He reached out to touch Pauly's face, cupping his chiseled jaw, praying it wouldn't be long before Pauly figured out what he wanted. Figured out he wanted Sloane.

"I'm sure."

"Pauly, I lo—"

"No, don't. We want different things right now, so just go. Be happy."

13

"Be happy? What the fuck, man? You're acting like we'll never see each other again. I just want to spend New Year's away from Nashville."

"And I want to stay here, so see? Different things."

Sloane gripped the back of Pauly's head, pulling him in for a kiss. There was no way he was leaving things as they were. Pauly stood stiffly, unwilling to open for him. Instead, he placed both hands on Sloane's chest and pushed hard enough to break the connection.

"Look, just take some time with your wife and kid. Figure your shit out." Pauly turned and headed for the bathroom. Before he closed the door, he turned back and said, "You know where I'll be."

"She hasn't been my wife for a long fucking time, and you know it." What the fuck was that all about? Pauly didn't respond, so Sloane had no recourse but to do as his best friend said. He would hit the road, and hopefully with a little distance, Pauly would miss what they had together and reach out. If not? Sloane had no idea what he'd do if he lost Pauly completely. Pulling up the Uber app, Sloane called for a car to take him to the airport. With one last look around the hotel room where he and Pauly had christened almost every usable surface, he let himself out, leaving the keycard on the table.

***

PAULY LEANED HIS hands against the bathroom counter, his

14

head bowed. When he heard the snick of the hotel door closing, he let out a deep sigh. It took everything in him not to run after Sloane, but he loved his best friend too much to stand in the way of his happiness. Being around Tag and Erik, seeing them being a family, must have taken hold in Sloane. Hearing Sloane admit as much to Tag had been a hard pill to swallow. If Sloane wanted to be a family with Tracy and Taryn, he wouldn't stand in the way. The thing he didn't understand was Sloane hadn't mentioned his ex or daughter in a long time. Whenever Pauly had thought of having a family, he'd always considered it would be him and Sloane going forward.

Pauly had already decided to reconnect with his own kids, or at least try. But he'd thought he and Sloane would do that together. Thought they'd write songs together and maybe play locally for a while. He had no interest in his house in Malibu. That was something he'd needed at the height of their career in 7's Mistress. That, the fancy sports cars, the all-night parties. Pauly wanted a slower-paced life now that he could have it. Years spent traveling the world selling out the largest arenas was what every musician dreamed of. They had lived the dream. Now, though, Pauly had different dreams. Ones of him and Sloane settling down together. Yes, he wanted it in Nashville where he could be around the others.

Mack and Gus were planning to open their own security company in Nashville since Mack and Bethany were together,

15

and Gus went where Mack did. Just because the band had broken up didn't mean they all had to scatter. Heart heavy, Pauly returned to the living room and picked up his guitar. The song Sloane caught him playing was supposed to be a surprise. Pauly didn't usually write lyrics, just the melody, but words had been floating around his head as he strummed. Words of promise, love, and a future. Guess he could put that one on the back burner for the time being.

With Sloane gone, the large hotel suite was oppressive. His plans to spend New Years alone with Sloane a fading dream. He wasn't ready to go back to Tag's, because he didn't want to ruin the holiday spirit that was alive and well in their home. Hell, even Mack had found love with Bethany and her baby boy. Maybe Pauly should try to reconnect with his kids instead of building a new family with Sloane or butting into Tag's life just so he could be around Delilah. He wasn't trying to use the little princess to replace his own kids. Was he?

Fuck.

He went in search of his phone, stopping at the door to the bedroom where he'd spent the last few weeks with Sloane. The bed was rumpled, and the sheets were twisted as they usually were after a night wrapped around each other. Except when they were sleeping on the bus, the two of them had shared the same bed every night for many years, and knowing he wouldn't have that now was enough to choke him. He swiped the tears off his cheeks, striding over to the side he slept on, and grabbed his phone off the nightstand where it was charging. Before he left the room, Pauly leaned over and picked up the pillow on the opposite side. Shoving his nose in the white cotton, he inhaled deeply. Instead of feeling better, Pauly's heart stuttered when Sloane's scent invaded his senses. Why the fuck had he let the best part of him walk out the door?

Go after him.

And do what? Tell him he can't get back together with his ex? Can't be a father to his daughter? That would be selfish. Pauly should worry about his own kids. Reach out and do more than sending cards on their birthdays and Christmas, and calling a few times a year. Dammit! He hadn't sent a card to them this year. He'd been so caught up in everything Sloane and Delilah, he'd completely forgotten. It wasn't like he was going to win father of the year anyway. Taking his phone back to the living room, he dropped down on the sofa and pulled up the number to his daughter, Juno, but then he remembered it was too early on the West Coast to call. Both kids still lived in California, so he needed to wait until later so he wouldn't wake them.

With nothing better to do, Pauly decided to shower and go back to Tag's for a while. He knew he was intruding on their time, but the way he saw it, he could watch Delilah and give them time to do whatever they wanted as a couple. If they didn't want him there, he'd figure out something else. After

17

showering, he left the hotel, stopping to grab some donuts before heading to their home.

***

WHILE SLOANE WAITED to board the plane, he decided to call his ex. "Now's not a good time, Sloane," Tracy answered.

"What's wrong?"

"Other than our house burning down last week? Nothing," she huffed.

"What the fuck, Tracy?" Sloane heard the gasp from the woman sitting next to him, but he couldn't be bothered to care. Not with the bombshell his ex just dropped on him.

"Don't 'what the fuck,' me, Sloane. If you cared anything about Taryn at all, you would have already known this."

Sloane stood, grabbed his bag, and walked toward the bathrooms where he'd have more privacy. He had already caught several cameras snapping pictures of him. He didn't need his private life videotaped and shared on social media. "Do not do that. You know I love my kid, and I just talked to her a couple weeks ago. The phone works both ways."

"Well, like I said, now's not a good time," Tracy's voice wavered. She was tough as nails when she needed to be, but having their home burn down had to have been devastating.

"Where are you?" Sloane leaned against the wall with his back to all the travelers passing by him to get to their

18

respective gates.

"We're staying at Derik's parents' for now."

"Don't they have a two-bedroom house?" Taryn had told him about visiting her new set of grandparents. With Tracy's parents living on the East Coast and Sloane's family not caring enough to act like grandparents, it made sense Taryn would latch onto Derik's parents. His daughter wasn't materialistic at all, but she had mentioned how small the house was.

"Yes, but at least we aren't living in a hotel."

"I wish you'd have called me. The beach house is empty. I'm actually headed there now to grab a few things, but it's yours for as long as you need it." Tracy was quiet, and Sloane looked at his phone to make sure he hadn't lost her.

The sound of a door closing came across the line, and then she was back. "Are you serious?"

"Of course. I know you and I didn't work out, but that doesn't mean I don't care about you. Besides, Taryn's my daughter. I'll always provide for her financially even if I suck at the other stuff. The band broke up, so maybe I'll work on the other stuff too, if she'll let me."

"I'll need to talk to Derik, but that would be wonderful if we could hang out at your place for a while."

"Do you want me to talk to him?" Sloane had no problem with Tracy's new husband. From what Taryn told Sloane, Derik was good to her, and that's all that mattered.

"No, I'll do it. If he agrees, when can we move in?"

19

"As soon as you can get there. My flight is set to take off in thirty minutes. I'll be there in about five hours."

"I'll talk to Derik, and then I'll call you back."

"Okay. I'll be waiting."

Sloane disconnected and closed his eyes. He'd never felt more like shit than he did in that moment. His kid's home had burned down and he hadn't had a clue. He'd seen the fires on the news, but it never crossed his mind his family could have been affected. While he waited, Sloane put in a call to his sister and asked her to get the beach house ready. He already knew Tracy would take him up on his offer, because he knew how much she loved their daughter.

Even though they were both from Tennessee, Sloane's baby sister moved to California after high school looking for her big break in the movies. While Syd got some commercial work and bit parts in sitcoms, she never made it big. It never stopped her from taking the small roles, and she'd made a name for herself as that actor whose face you recognized if not their name. While she wasn't auditioning, Sloane paid her to take care of his house. Just as he hung up with Syd, Tracy called back accepting his offer. He couldn't rebuild his kid's home, but he could make her life a little bit better for the time being.

Chapter Three

"GOOD MORNING," ERIK said when he opened the door. Duke pushed past his owner and sat at Pauly's feet, leaning against his leg. "Is everything okay?" Erik asked, looking behind Pauly.

"Why wouldn't it be?" Pauly didn't really want to go into great detail of why he was on their doorstep so early.

Erik stepped back, and Pauly entered the living room with Duke on his heels. When he closed the door, Erik said, "Several reasons. One, you walked out without Sloane yesterday. Two, you're here without Sloane this morning. And three, Duke is keeping you close. If the first two weren't indicators, he is letting me know you aren't in the best of moods."

"Pauly?" Tag said as he came down the hall with Delilah in his arms. "What's wrong?"

Pauly huffed out a laugh. "I guess you aren't going to believe I just wanted to see Delilah?"

"No. Now, hand over the donuts. You take the princess, and I'll start coffee." Tag held the baby out to Pauly, and once he handed the box over to Erik, Pauly took Delilah and held

21

her close, sniffing her neck. He loved the smell of baby lotion.

"Okay, coffee will be ready in a few minutes. Until then, spill," Tag urged as he returned from the kitchen, sitting next to Erik on the sofa.

Pauly took the recliner and rocked Delilah while she grabbed at his long hair. "Sloane left."

"And you didn't go with him?" Erik asked. The doctor had been around long enough to know the two were always together.

"He wants his family back, and I won't get in the way."

"I don't understand why he would tell you that," Tag said, sliding to the edge of the sofa, elbows on his knees.

Pauly cleared his throat so he could choke out the words. "I overheard the two of you talking yesterday. He wants his family, and that isn't me. He said he needed to get away, so I had to let him go."

"That's not..." Tag shook his head, letting the comment die.

"What is it you want?" Erik asked.

"I thought he and I would continue making music together. I want to stay here in Nashville to be close to you all."

"And you're sure he doesn't want the same thing?" Tag asked.

"He said he needed to get away, so yeah, pretty sure." *Even though he almost said he loved you?* Pauly had no idea

22

what to think.

"For what it's worth, the two of you have been close for fifteen years. If anyone knows Sloane, really knows him, it's you. Don't let miscommunication get in the way of what could be something good," Tag said softly. He rose and headed to the kitchen. When he returned, he had coffee for all of them along with a plate of donuts. Pauly chose a glazed one, leaving the sprinkles and chocolate-covered for Tag and Erik. He'd become adept at eating one-handed with the baby in his lap, but he didn't touch the coffee for fear of spilling the hot liquid on her.

As he held Delilah close, he didn't miss the looks Tag and Erik gave each other. Silent conversations only they understood. He had that with Sloane, and in that moment, he knew he would do anything to keep it, even if it meant baring his soul to his best friend. If Sloane wanted a family, Pauly would be the one to give it to him. He just had to convince his lover they were meant to be together.

"I need to go," he said abruptly, standing while cradling Delilah to his chest. He kissed her on her chubby cheek. "Uncle Pauly is on a mission, Princess."

Tag and Erik grinned, and Erik reached out for the baby. "Go get your man."

Pauly hugged his friends. "I'm not sure when I'll be back, so I'll go ahead and wish you both a happy New Year."

"Call if you need us. For anything," Tag said, clapping

23

Pauly's back when they hugged. Pauly nodded and let himself out of the house.

Sliding into the driver's seat of the rental, Pauly settled back, gripping the steering wheel tightly. He had no idea where Sloane was, but the first place Pauly was going to look was in LA. He didn't bother going back to the hotel. It was paid for through the end of the year, so he opened his phone and booked the first flight to California he could get and then headed to the airport.

His flight didn't leave for a couple hours, and that gave Pauly too much time to think. He had nothing with him. No clothes, no guitar, and nothing to write on. Instead of sitting with the mass of travelers, he found a quiet spot in the smoking lounge. He'd given up cigarettes a long time ago, but the small room offered him a modicum of privacy. He opened an app on his phone and typed in some lyrics that had been floating around his head. Pauly already had the tune down, and now that the words were flowing, he knew it would be a love song of sorts for his man.

Flying first class helped with fans leaving him alone during the flight, but he was stopped several times while walking toward the exit. When the plane touched down, it was only three in the afternoon California time. Pauly didn't bother with an Uber or calling for a car service, instead opting for one of the waiting taxis. While in route to his secluded home, Pauly sent Sloane a text asking where he was. If he wasn't in

Malibu, Pauly would turn around and travel to wherever Sloane was. Pauly was almost home by the time his phone pinged with a return message.

Sloane: *At the beach house*

Pauly considered telling the taxi driver to change directions, but he had nothing with him, and knowing Sloane was close by was good enough for a couple more hours. He needed to go home first to pack a bag and grab one of his guitars. Plus, that would give him time to work on the song he'd written. Even though it was for Sloane, Pauly had written it with harmonies in mind. He and his best friend sang well together. They did a lot of things well together, and he wasn't ready to give that up.

***

WHILE SLOANE WAITED on Pauly to send another text, he and Syd sat around the living room with Tracy, Taryn, and Derik. It took every bit of will power in him not to check his phone every fifteen seconds. Syd had outdone herself in decorating the whole downstairs on such short notice with a Christmas tree and all the trimmings. In all the years Sloane was with Pauly, Tag, and Cade, they'd never really exchanged gifts, other than a bottle of liquor here and there. They'd never shared the holiday like they had this year, and it made Sloane wish for more of the same in the future.

25

Sloane wished he could have convinced Pauly to come to California with him, but it didn't seem like they were on the same page at the moment. Instead of dwelling on what he couldn't have, he focused on what he could give his daughter. Technically, Christmas was over, but that didn't mean they couldn't continue to celebrate. And if anyone needed a reason to take their mind off life for a while, it was Sloane's ex and kid.

Christmastime in Malibu was completely different than in Tennessee. When Sloane left Nashville, the weather had been cold and threatening snow. Now, he was wearing a short-sleeved tee and was barefoot. The doors to the patio were open, and a nice breeze was blowing in off the ocean. Since Syd didn't know what kind of food everyone liked, she'd bought stuff to grill both burgers and steaks. Things had been awkward at first, especially with Derik, but when the other man figured out Sloane wasn't trying to win his family back, he chilled. Then, he thanked Sloane at least ten times for taking them in, and the two of them settled into some good conversations.

"You should play for your dad," Tracy told Taryn when they stopped off in the music room. Taryn blushed, but she bit her lip and waited to see if Sloane agreed.

"Play what?" Sloane asked.

"I have a surprise for you," she said. He expected his daughter to go to the keyboard, but she shocked him, picking

26

up one of his guitars. Derik appeared in the door, and Tracy excused herself to go help him with the burgers. Sloane figured it was an excuse to give the two of them some alone time.

"So, show me what you've got," Sloane urged, and after making sure his thousand-dollar rhythm guitar was in tune, she played one of 7's Mistress's older songs. Like a pro.

Sloane picked up his bass, and together, the two of them got lost in song after song. Taryn missed notes here and there, but the way her fingers glided over the strings with ease meant she'd been playing a while. She was damn good for a twelve-year-old, and Sloane couldn't be prouder. He lent his voice to the music, and when he urged his daughter to sing along, she shook her head.

"You really don't want me singing," she said, laughing.

"It can't be that bad," Sloane argued.

"Okay, you asked for it." She strummed the intro to "Deliver Me," and Sloane sang the first verse. When Taryn came in on harmonies, or tried to, he grinned but didn't stop the song to tell her she was right. As good as she was on guitar, her voice really was awful.

When Tracy came back into the room, she announced the food was ready. He hadn't realized how hungry he was until his stomach growled. Sloane slung an arm around Taryn's neck as they walked down the long hallway to the patio doors. "You're really good," he told her.

27

Taryn beamed at his praise. "Thanks. It's all I've ever been interested in. Plus, when your dad's this world-famous rock star, everyone sort of expects you to have some of the same abilities. I figured since I loved music, I might as well prove them right."

"I used some of the money you sent on soundproofing the garage," Tracy said. "She wasn't always this good, and the neighbors didn't appreciate having a rock star wannabe next door."

"Well, you're not a wannabe any longer. You're better than a lot of guys out on the road," Sloane told Taryn.

"Yeah, right." She shook her head, but Sloane didn't miss the smile she tried to hide.

"Who'd you get to teach you?"

"I watched YouTube videos." Taryn shrugged as if teaching herself to play was no big deal.

"No shit? Damn, girl. If you had a professional give you lessons, there's no telling how much you'd grow your craft."

"If I only knew a professional," she deadpanned.

"Pauly would be perfect. He's the most talented guitarist I know."

"I was talking about you," she said, bumping into his hip with hers.

"Maybe, but there's not a better guitarist out there than Les Paulson."

"Speaking of Pauly, he stopped by earlier," Tracy said.

28

"That's impossible. He's in Nashville."

"Sloane, I think I know who Pauly is. He came by earlier. I told him you and Taryn were in the music room and he should join you. He got a funny look on his face and took off."

"What the hell?" Sloane asked more to himself than his ex. Pauly was here? In Malibu? "I need to make a call. Please go ahead and start eating." Sloane left the others to their own devices as he headed back inside to find his phone. He expected there to be either a missed call or at the least another text from Pauly, but there was nothing. He pulled up his favorites and hit Pauly's name. When the call connected, it went straight to voicemail. "Dude, what the fuck? You come all this way and don't come in the house? Call me."

He tried calling again with the same result. Instead of leaving another message, he sent a text.

Sloane: *Call me.*

Sloane: *Please?*

What the ever-loving hell was Pauly's deal? He said he wanted to stay in Nashville, and then he comes to California anyway. It didn't make any sense. Sloane didn't have time to contemplate what his lover was thinking. After ensuring his phone was set to ring and not vibrate, Sloane returned to the patio. Even though he was no longer hungry, he didn't want to be rude. While fixing a plate, Sloane asked Tracy, "Did Pauly say why he was here?"

"No. He looked really surprised to see me open the door.

29

I apologize for that, by the way. I probably shouldn't have, but I did look through the peephole first. Since it was him, I figured it'd be okay."

"Of course, it's okay. You're living here now, so you can open the door whenever you want, unless it's the paparazzi. Then I'd suggest you run the other way."

Tracy rolled her eyes. "Anyway, whenever I told him you and Taryn were in the music room, he almost looked like I'd kicked his puppy. He said it was good to see me, and then he just left."

The only thing Sloane could think of was Pauly was jealous. After the comment he made about Sloane going back to his wife… And now, that's probably exactly what he thought, that Sloane had run home to Malibu and moved Tracy and Taryn in. Pauly didn't know the truth. Rarely did he and Pauly talk about their kids, and whenever Sloane talked with Taryn, he didn't share the subjects of their conversations. Never felt the need to. If he'd only told Pauly Tracy had remarried. Sloane really needed to find him.

"I'm sure he's fine. I'll catch up with him later," Sloane lied. He did his best to not let on his heart was about to burst out of his chest at the thought of Pauly thinking Sloane didn't want him. He wanted nothing more than the two of them to be together, and Sloane was in it for the long haul. Had been for a while.

Once they finished eating, Syd had to take off for work,

so Sloane encouraged his three houseguests to make themselves at home. For about the twentieth time, he assured both Tracy and Derik it was no imposition, and he had plenty of room. Now he knew Pauly was in town, Sloane was on a mission to find his best friend and figure out what was going through his head. He would pack a bag and go stay with his lover, giving everyone their own space. Since Pauly wouldn't return his call, Sloane pulled out the big guns.

"Sloane, what's shaking?" Echo asked when the line connected. "You and Pauly ready to sign a contract?" The woman had been their manager for 7's Mistress, and she was eager to continue with at least two of the four of the band.

"Not exactly. I need your help. Pauly's not answering my call, and I really need to get hold of him." After a little prodding on Echo's part, Sloane explained what happened that morning at the hotel and afterward when Pauly arrived at the beach house. "I really need to talk to him."

"Let me see what I can do, and I'll call you back."

Sloane went to his room, doing his best to avoid Tracy and Derik. He wouldn't mind spending time with Taryn, but he had opened his house to them as a place to stay after their tragedy. He wasn't going to make things awkward by insinuating himself into their interactions. If Taryn wanted to talk to him, she would find him. He packed a suitcase with enough clothes for a week. He added a few items from his bedside drawer he and Pauly could enjoy together. Then, he

31

began pacing. He opened the French doors in his bedroom and stepped out onto the patio which overlooked the ocean. He'd owned his house for over ten years, and he'd only seen the view from this perspective a handful of times. What a waste.

Taking a seat in one of the cushioned chairs, Sloane propped his feet on the railing and threaded his fingers together across his stomach. He loved the beach. The waves crashing as they broke, the seagulls circling overhead, the salty aroma that wafted on the wind. As much as he loved the area, Sloane no longer needed the large house or the flashy red sports car, if he were being honest with himself. He was glad to have somewhere Taryn could stay until her mom and stepdad got back on their feet, but after that? That was one of the things he wanted to talk to Pauly about. Living together. Making music together. Having a family together. He would give it all up to live in a shack with his lover if that's what it took for them to have a future.

It was a couple hours before Sloane heard back from Echo. He was still sitting on the patio when he answered the phone.

"That boy's all kinds of messed up over you. I didn't tell him the truth of why I reached out to him, because I figured that needed to come from you. If you want to talk to Pauly, show up at Rooster's tonight. There's a special guest playing there around ten."

"A special guest, huh? Was that your doing?" Sloane

asked, already knowing the answer.

"Maybe. Jackson Cane has been trying to get hold of you guys for years, and while it isn't the whole band, he jumped at the chance to have any one of you show up for an impromptu set."

"Didn't Pauly ask how you knew he was in Cali?"

"Sure did, and I told him he was trending. Y'all can't fly commercial without photos showing up on social media. Just so you know, you're trending as well, so look out for the leeches." That was Echo's term for paparazzi. Sloane had gotten used to having cameras stuck in his face a long time ago. It came with the territory.

"Thanks for the heads-up, and thanks especially for getting Pauly the gig. I have an idea of how to get him to talk to me afterwards. Please call Jackson back and let him know I'll be there right at ten. If he can sneak me in the back, that'd be great."

"You're welcome, and I'm on it. I wish I was in the area. I would love to see you on stage together. You two are truly magic."

"If things go my way, there will be plenty of future magic for you to partake in."

Echo sighed. "I sure hope so. Text me tomorrow and let me know how it goes."

"Will do. Love you, spitfire."

"Love you, too."

Sloane glanced at the clock. It was too early to head down to the club, and with the time difference, it felt later than it was, so Sloane closed the patio doors and pulled the black-out curtains together. He set his alarm and lay down for a nap. By the time the chime sounded, he was well rested and ready to see what the night would bring. One way or another, he and Pauly were going to hash out everything between them, and Sloane meant everything.

Sloane called for a car service to take him to Rooster's. The company was one which was used to dealing with high-profile customers, and the drivers were always courteous and professional. Being accustomed to having stars in their backseats meant Sloane didn't have to worry about a star-struck person talking nonstop or asking for autographs and selfies.

After taking a shower, Sloane lined his eyes with kohl, painted his nails black, and dressed in tight black jeans and a black, nearly sheer button-up. Instead of piling his long, blond hair up in a bun, he brushed it out, letting it fall around his shoulders the way Pauly liked it. Lastly, he spritzed Pauly's favorite cologne into the air and walked through it. Taking one last look in the mirror, Sloane said goodbye to his houseguests and headed to Rooster's.

Chapter Four

PAULY NEVER COULD say no to Echo, and playing in front of people was what he thrived on, even if it wasn't an arena filled with twenty thousand fans. A small crowd was the perfect venue to showcase the latest songs he'd written to gauge their interest in the new sound. Jackson Cane had been trying to get 7's Mistress to play Rooster's for many years. He wasn't getting the band, but Echo assured Pauly that Jackson was just as eager to have one member, especially now the band had broken up. Seeing any one of them continuing to play gave the fans the band's music. Gave them hope they hadn't truly heard the last of 7's Mistress.

Playing guitar and singing would take his mind off things even if just for a little while. He'd made the mistake of confiding in Echo why he was in California. He'd even confessed how he was torn up over Sloane being back with his ex. Pauly understood Sloane's need to be around Taryn; she was his kid, after all. Before Echo's call, Pauly finally got hold of both his own kids and apologized for the lack of a Christmas card, but he assured both he would see them soon and try to make up for lost time. Les Jr. seemed more thrilled

35

than Juno, but his son had always thought having a rock star for a father was the shit. Then again, the kid was only ten.

Both Corinne and Dana, his kids' mothers, had agreed to his seeing Juno and Les Jr. They knew Pauly loved his kids, even if he hadn't been there for all the milestones. He promised both he planned to do better in the future now that he wasn't going to be on the road constantly.

Pauly dressed in torn jeans and a black T-shirt. He popped his fedora on his head, grabbed his favorite acoustic guitar – the one he didn't take on the road – and then headed out. He would get there early, but having a couple drinks before he took the stage would take the edge off his nerves. What he wouldn't give to have Sloane joining him for a duet. The two of them had made some beautiful music together over the years, but it didn't seem like that was in the cards for the immediate future.

Jackson Cane was waiting at the back door for Pauly. He welcomed him with an outstretched hand and a straight, white smile. If Pauly was into older men with stylish salt and pepper hair and striking blue eyes, Jackson would fit the bill. Pauly's heart belonged to a tall, thin blond with hazel eyes who knew him inside and out.

"Pauly, come in. I can't thank you enough for playing tonight."

"It's my pleasure. I love the crowds, no matter how large or small." And that was the truth. Pauly just loved playing

36

guitar. He wasn't as thrilled about singing, but he had a decent enough voice that the fans would forgive him for not sounding like Tag.

"I've prepared the dressing room. Is there anything I can get for you?" With a hand at the small of his back, Jackson ushered Pauly to a private room that was small but clean and set up with new-looking furniture. Most of the smaller places he'd played over the years had been equipped with folding chairs or sofas that looked like they'd been picked up off the side of the road. At least this room was brightly lit and bigger than a broom closet. As well as being neat, there was a bouquet of flowers on the dressing table. Pauly wondered if those were for him or just the usual decoration.

"I'd love a drink, but I have no problem going to the bar."

"Nonsense. You're practically royalty, so please, let me treat you as such. Just tell me what you want and I'll see to it you're taken care of all night." Jackson Cane was pouring on the charm, and if Pauly didn't know better, he was acting like more than just a bar owner. He was a fan, too, but there was a certain gleam in his eye that Pauly thought might have been interest. Would it hurt if the man was flirting with him? Yes, it would. Pauly wasn't going to believe the last years with Sloane meant so little he'd so quickly give up on what they had.

But he'd already done that. Hadn't he?

"Pauly?" Jackson asked, bringing his attention back to the

handsome man standing in front of him. Pauly was tall, but Jackson had a few inches on him, plus the man was broad. Pauly had never given much thought to what type of man, or woman, he was attracted to. They either caught his eye or they didn't. For the last several years, he'd never considered taking anyone to bed other than Sloane. It seemed his dick was still on the Sloane train, since it wasn't twitching in the least under his tight jeans.

"I'll take a Jack and Coke. But you don't have to cater to me."

"It's no trouble at all. You settle in, and I'll be right back."

Alone in the room, Pauly set his case down and pulled his guitar out. He knew it was already tuned, but he plucked at the strings anyway. He was going over the latest song he'd been working on when a knock sounded.

"Come in," Pauly called out, expecting it to be Jackson. A pretty blonde with huge tits spilling over her low-cut Rooster's T-shirt came in holding a tray.

"Hello Mr. Paulson. I'm Jess. Jackson asked that I see to your needs tonight," she said, looking Pauly over like he was a lollipop and she wanted to lick him. "I brought a set-up so you can have more than one drink, if you wish. Also, I grabbed some snacks in case you're hungry."

Pauly was surprised Jackson had sent someone else, but he did have a bar to run. "Thank you, Jess. And please, call me Pauly. Mr. Paulson was my father."

"Okay, Pauly." After setting the tray on the table, Jess filled the rocks glass with ice from the bucket before adding a strong serving of whiskey followed by a dash of Coke. He appreciated the fact that she was trying to give him good service and not skimping on the alcohol, but Pauly only wanted to take the edge off, not get drunk. If this had been back when the band first started, he'd have just chugged from the bottle.

"You can set that down," he said, indicating the glass. He wouldn't hurt her feelings by pouring it out in front of her. "I'm going to warm my fingers up first."

"Is there anything else I can do for you?" Jess bit her bottom lip. She was a beautiful woman, and the gesture would have caught his interest at one time, but not any longer.

"I'm good. Just please close the door behind you when you leave."

Jess's smile faltered only a couple seconds before it was back in place. "I'll be here all night," she said before walking out of the room with a little added swing in her hips. Pauly had to give her aces for trying. Instead of drinking what Jess had poured for him, Pauly dumped out half the drink into a fresh glass and added more Coke on top of what was left. He sipped the new mixture, letting the alcohol calm his nerves. He wasn't anxious about playing. He was still dealing with the sadness of finding Sloane's ex at his door.

Another knock on the door pulled him out of his musings.

39

"Five minutes 'til showtime," a strange voice called out without coming inside.

Pauly didn't realize how long he'd sat there holding his guitar in one hand and the half-empty Jack and Coke in the other. Downing the rest of it, Pauly set the empty glass down, took a deep breath, and called out, "I'm ready." He didn't bother checking his appearance in the mirror. Being a rock star afforded him the forgiveness of the crowd if he looked like shit. They were there to hear him play 7's Mistress songs, and if he looked worse for the wear, they would chalk it up to the "lifestyle."

Grabbing a bottle of water and his guitar, Pauly opened the door and followed the stranger down the hallway to the back of the stage. Jackson was waiting for him. "I'll introduce you, and then it's all yours," the man said. His smile was even bigger than when he'd introduced himself at the back door. Maybe he hadn't been flirting. Maybe, he was just happy to have such a huge name playing his establishment. If word got out Pauly was there, he had no doubt the place would be packed.

When he took the stage, he found out he wasn't wrong. It was standing room only. Unlike large arenas where the lights were so bright you couldn't see the crowd, Rooster's was bright and well-lit, but Pauly could make out everyone out in front of him. Tag, being the lead singer, had always been the spokesman for the band. This was something new for Pauly,

40

but he took a deep breath and found his voice.

"Hello, and thank you all for coming out tonight." The crowd cheered and whistled for him. Pauly gave them a moment to settle down before speaking again. "As Jackson so graciously said, I'm Les Paulson, lead guitarist for 7's Mistress. If you've seen us play over the years, you know I'm only a back-up singer, so I'll warn you now, I'm no Taggart Lee, but I hope to entertain you anyway. If you know the words, feel free to sing along."

Pauly played an hour straight, pulling from the band's extensive catalog. He sang his heart out while the crowd did the same. He finished the set with a cover of an old Jimmy Hendrix classic, and the crowd was on their feet.

"I'm going to take a short break, and then I'll be back with another set. While I'm gone, be sure to refill those glasses, and don't forget to take care of the wait staff. I've been watching them all night, and they're definitely taking care of you."

Jackson Cane met him at the microphone, his smile lighting up the room. "Give it up for Les Paulson!" Jackson let the ovation go on for a moment, and Pauly left the man to do whatever it was the owner of a club needed to between sets. Pauly had just taken a few steps down the hallway toward the dressing room when Jackson's voice boomed, "I told you this night would be full of surprises, didn't I? If you thought that was a treat, I have another for you!"

41

Pauly had just reached the dressing room when Jackson announced, "What's better than one member of 7's Mistress? Try two! While Pauly takes a break, I'm proud to introduce to you Sloane Vargus, bass player for the band. Sloane, come on out here!" The last sentence was almost drowned out by the crowd cheering. Surely, he'd heard Jackson wrong. There was no way Sloane was there. Pauly headed back toward the stage, meeting Jackson halfway down the hallway.

"Did I hear you right?" Pauly asked when he was standing in front of the owner.

"That your pal Sloane is here?" Jackson nodded and gestured toward the stage. "See for yourself."

Pauly strode past the man and stopped short when he caught sight of Sloane taking the stool Pauly had minutes ago vacated.

"What's up, Rooster's?" Sloane had no trouble playing to the crowd. "Give it up one more time for my best friend, Les Paulson!" When the fans calmed somewhat, Sloane strummed his own acoustic guitar. "Pauly didn't know I was going to be here tonight, and I don't want to infringe on his set. I'm gonna play a couple songs while he's on break, and then maybe he'll let me join him on stage. The two of us make a pretty good team, if I do say so myself."

After more yells, whistles, and clapping, Sloane strummed his guitar and settled into "Divine Intervention." It was one of the first songs he wrote for the band, and he and

42

Pauly had spent hours perfecting it. Sloane's voice wasn't as smooth as Pauly's. It had a rasp to it Pauly always found sexy as fuck. If he wasn't so confused by Sloane being there, he would have probably been sporting a hard-on. Surely Sloane wouldn't leave Tracy alone on their first night back together. Thinking that, Pauly scanned the crowd.

When Jackson stepped up beside him, he asked the man, "What's he doing here?"

"Said he wanted to surprise you."

"Me?"

"By the look on your face, I'd say it worked. I don't know much about your friendship, but when he called me earlier, he practically begged for the opportunity to play tonight."

"He called you." It was a statement, one Pauly was trying to work through. How had…? Echo. Of course, the little minx would have called Sloane and told him what was going on. That would teach him to ever confide in her again. He'd poured his heart out, and she turned around and told Sloane where to find him.

When the applause died down after Sloane's first song, he said, "I would like to ask you all to indulge me for a moment. I know 7's Mistress has twelve albums filled with hit songs, but I'd like to do a cover that means a lot to me." Pauly had no idea which song Sloane was about to play, but it wasn't long until he recognized Lenny Kravitz's "Can't Get You Off My Mind." Pauly's eyes misted, and his throat tightened.

Pauly had drunkenly played it one night for Sloane, telling him it was how he felt whenever they were apart for any length of time. There was no way Sloane was playing it for him this time. Not with... Sloane turned toward the side of the stage and sang the chorus directly to Pauly.

Well, fuck.

Chapter Five

SLOANE HAD NO idea if singing to Pauly would get his point across. If not, he'd have a conversation with his lover after the show. When he looked over to where Pauly was standing with Jackson Cane, he could've sworn he saw Pauly brushing a tear from his cheek. He hadn't intended for his best friend to become that emotional. He only wanted him to know Sloane was his. Nobody else's. When the song was over, he smiled at Pauly in a way he doubted he ever had before. It was with as much love as he could impart into just a look. Pauly blinked hard a couple times before smiling back.

Sloane stood from the stool, not bothering to address the cheering fans. He strode toward Pauly and met him halfway across the stage. When they reached one another, Sloane pulled him into his arms. They didn't kiss. Didn't say anything, just held one another to more whistles and catcalls. This wasn't the time for Sloane to pour his heart out to Pauly any more than he already had with the song. They had screaming fans to entertain, so he pulled away and asked, "Care if I join you up here?"

"I'd be honored," Pauly said. Jackson Cane walked onto

the stage carrying an extra stool, while one of his employees set up an extra microphone stand.

When they were seated, Pauly held up his hand. "This is just as much a surprise to me as it is to all of you. We haven't rehearsed a set, so please bear with us."

Sloane wasn't worried about the crowd, or his and Pauly's lack of rehearsing as a duet. The two of them had spent countless hours in their downtime with just the two of them playing. Their harmonies were usually spot-on. Tonight was basically a free concert for the patrons at Rooster's, so if he and Pauly weren't perfect, the folks could ask for their fucking money back. He was there for Pauly and nobody else.

Pauly took control just as Sloane had known he would, and the night went smoothly. They played several 7's Mistress's songs as well as some well-known covers. When they told the crowd they had one more song to play, Pauly surprised Sloane. "As you all know, the band recently parted ways since Taggart Lee decided to become domesticated." The crowd groaned, and some even booed. "He's lived the rock star life for fifteen years, and now he's settled down with the love of his life and their beautiful baby girl." That garnered a room full of awws.

"I've been working on some new material. It doesn't have the same vibe your used to from our band, but that's the great thing about music and artists. Both evolve. Sloane, here, has heard the melody, but I only added the lyrics this morning

46

while waiting on my flight from Tennessee. I might forget some of the words, so if I do, please forgive me. This one's called 'The Road Home.'"

Nameless faces in nameless towns
Time keeps passing by
Empty bottles in empty rooms
The nights stretch out in a blur

A mile at a time with no end in sight
It looks like I'll never get home
A mile at a time leading farther away
I need help finding my way home

Thousands of people and thousands of hours
Nothing fills the void
Looking for peace and looking for love
Is impossible for someone like me

A mile at a time with no end in sight
It seems like I'll never get home
A mile at a time leading farther away
I need help finding my way home

Reaching for you, always reaching for you
My elusive star in the sky

47

Calling your name, calling out with my heart
You're walking a different path

A mile at a time with no end in sight
I'm searching for the road home
A mile at a time leading farther away
I need to find my road home

A mile at a time please come hold my hand
Together we'll find the road home
A mile at a time I need you with me
Don't you know Baby, you are my home

Sloane recognized the tune as the one Pauly had been playing at the hotel. He didn't know the whole tune, so instead of strumming along, he sat and enjoyed the same show the fans were getting – Les Paulson in all his glory. As Pauly's words washed over Sloane, he was now the one trying to keep the tears at bay. His man had written those words that morning, thinking he'd lost his chance with Sloane. Sloane needed to find out what led Pauly to believe Sloane didn't want him any longer. Pauly sang the last verse with his eyes glued to Sloane, and when it was done, Pauly closed his eyes, but not before Sloane saw the hurt buried there.

Sloane had to get Pauly alone to talk. When the last chord was strummed, Sloane stood from his stool and placed his guitar against the stand before pulling Pauly's from his hands, setting it aside as well. He grabbed Pauly's hand, holding it above their heads, and the two of them took a bow as if they were in a jam-packed arena. When the people rose from their seats and began heading toward the stage, Sloane practically dragged Pauly down the hallway toward the dressing room. Jackson Cane had shown Sloane the room earlier so he had somewhere to leave his guitar case. He also explained the two of them would be able to use it as a place to hide after the show, since there hadn't been time to add extra security.

Once inside the room, Sloane pushed Pauly against the door and pressed their bodies together. Pauly was usually the one to be the aggressor, but Sloane knew he had one chance to get this right. He took Pauly's face in his hands and ghosted his lips across Pauly's. When Pauly let out a sigh, Sloane took advantage and kissed Pauly harder. Not a bruising crush of mouths, but a sensual tasting. It wasn't long before their dicks were hard. Sex wasn't something either one of them ever shied away from. After all their years together, they still got each other hot. It was the more intimate moments they weren't sure what to do with. Like the way they were kissing.

Pauly came up for breath and touched his forehead to Sloane's. "What are you doing here?"

"I thought that would have been apparent. I'm kissing you."

Pauly gripped Sloane's hips tightly. "I get that, but why

49

are you here, with me?"

"I'm not sure where the disconnect happened, but baby, you and I have been together, just the two of us, for a long time now. Why wouldn't I be here with you?" Sloane asked, pulling Pauly's fedora off his head and tossing it onto the nearby chair. He loved when Pauly wore hats, but in that moment, it was getting in the way.

Pauly tried to push Sloane away, but he didn't let him. "No. You don't get to push me away again. I should have stayed at the hotel and had this discussion earlier, but I was hurt and angry."

"I went to your house. Tracy was there."

"She told me. Why didn't you bother to come in?"

"I didn't want to intrude," Pauly confessed, his voice laced with pain. "I screwed up, and now you're back with her."

"Oh, babe. I guess I should've spent more time talking about personal shit with you instead of having porn-star sex and writing hit songs together. Tracy's remarried. Has been for a few years now. The reason they're at my house is because theirs burned down in the recent fires. There was no reason for them to live in a two-bedroom house with Derik's parents when I have my big, empty place."

"Well, fuck me," Pauly huffed.

"I've been trying for years, but you always like to be in charge." When they first started having sex, they switched

50

things up almost nightly, but after a while, Pauly fell into the more dominant roll, preferring to be on top.

Pauly laughed and pulled Sloane closer, nestling their erections together. Skinny jeans were hell on hard-ons. If things weren't so serious, Sloane would take them both in hand and give them some relief. Since he wanted to hash out what was going on between them, he kept his hands around Pauly's neck instead.

Pauly was still frowning. "I don't understand. I heard you and Tag talking about how you wanted a family. He mentioned Tracy and Taryn."

"If I recall, that was when you stormed out of the house. If you'd hung around a little longer, you'd have heard me tell him the truth. You're my family, Pauly. You're the man – the one – I want to be with now and for as long as you'll have me. We both have children of our own, and I think we need to spend some time reconnecting with them before we consider having one together, but it's something I've been thinking about."

"I thought you wanted away from Delilah. I thought that's why you left this morning. Well, yesterday morning." Since it was going on two a.m., it was the next day.

"God, it feels like I've lived a lifetime in those few hours. I left because I had hoped you and I could have some alone time, and when you said you wanted to stay in Nashville, I got pissed and ran. Don't get me wrong. I love Delilah, but we've

51

been spending all our spare time at Tag and Erik's. I was feeling a little left out, to be honest."

"We spend every night together."

Sloane promised himself he'd lay all his cards on the table. If Pauly didn't want him the way he wanted Pauly, now was the time to find out. "I want more. The sex is great, but I want what Tag and Erik have. I want a home with you. I want us to figure out our next steps as far as our music goes. And yes, I want to do that together. It's not like we haven't spent our lives in each other's pockets all these years. So, I'm not afraid of getting tired of one another. I want everything with you, Pauly. I love you."

"I love you too. You have to know that. Didn't you listen to the song I wrote for you?"

"I did listen, and I do know that now."

"But what if I want to make that life in Nashville? You don't want that." Pauly sighed, and Sloane knew this was the defining moment. He'd not considered making Tennessee a permanent home, but Nashville was the place for making music. Some of the biggest name producers had moved to the southern state, and now, Tag was going to become one of them. Who better to take charge of their career than their friend? Besides, he wanted to be where Pauly was.

"When I said I wanted to get out of Nashville, I only meant for a few days. We've been hanging out with the others every day, and I just wanted some alone time with you. As long as you make your life with me, I don't care where we live."

"Really?"

"Really. I planned on selling my house here, but I'm going to put that off until Tracy and Derik either rebuild or find another place to live. It's the least I can do for Taryn. We don't need two large houses on the West Coast."

"Then you'd be okay with me selling mine and looking for a place close to Nashville?"

"As long as it's a place for both of us, yeah. I'm good with it."

Pauly swung them around so he was the one pressing Sloane into the door. "I love you," he whispered before taking Sloane's lips in a scorching kiss. Pauly didn't have to urge Sloane to open up for him. He welcomed the heat and slide of Pauly's tongue as it traced every inch of Sloane's mouth. The kiss they shared just a few moments ago was one of hope. This one was all fire. It was the kind that led to things like clothes flying off and one of them ending up on their knees. In this case, it was Pauly. He dropped to the floor and had Sloane's leaking cock down his throat before Sloane knew what was happening.

Chapter Six

PAULY KNEW THINGS could turn on a dime. Between him and the other members of the band, life had taken them all on a rollercoaster ride. For the most part, their lives were all they could have ever dreamed of, but there were those times, like when Tag's sister had died, that life wasn't what they hoped it would be. Kneeling before Sloane sucking his cock, was just one of the better parts. Pauly knew it wasn't all about sex, but when the man you were in love with confessed his love as well as a promise for the future, it only added to the thrill. And sex with Sloane Vargus was always a thrill.

Tag had been right. Pauly's fears had stemmed from miscommunication. If he'd stuck around long enough to listen to the tail end of Sloane and Tag's conversation, his heart wouldn't have been torn in two. Then again, he wouldn't have written the song for Sloane he knew in his heart would become a number one hit for the right artist.

Pauly made fast work of sucking Sloane off. He wanted more with his man than a quick blowjob in the back of Rooster's. He wanted to take Sloane home and show him exactly what he meant to Pauly. As soon as Sloane blew his load down Pauly's throat, Pauly tucked Sloane back in his jeans. When he stood in front of Sloane, he said, "I hate to suck and run, be I need you in my bed." Sloane's current smile was one Pauly had seen plenty of times, the kind that said he was sated. Pauly vowed to see that smile every day for the rest of their lives. "Did you drive?" Pauly asked him.

"No. I didn't want to worry about my car getting dinged in the parking lot. Did you?"

"No. Same reason. Why don't you call for a ride, and I'll find Jackson and get our guitars?" Pauly ran a finger down Sloane's cheek. He couldn't believe this man was really his. Sure, they'd been together for years, but not in such a permanent way. There had never been talk of a future together. No plans for a home for just the two of them. No mention of one day having a child together. Pauly knew that particular dream was a way off, but at least it was a dream they shared.

Pauly returned from speaking with Jackson with both guitars in hand. After placing them in their respective cases, he noticed the suitcase at Sloane's feet. "Going somewhere?"

"I was hopeful this night would end with me at your house." Sloane grinned and shrugged.

The two men waited by the back door for their ride. Jackson had assured them he would run interference with the fans out front, giving them a story of how the two rock stars were possibly coming back out to sign autographs. Even though the back entrance to Rooster's was fenced and gated,

55

there were always those few fans who managed to slip through somehow. Lying to the masses was the least the owner could do to repay them for playing for free and drawing such a crowd. Before they'd parted ways, Pauly had promised to come back at a later date for another impromptu show.

Once seated in the backseat of the SUV Sloane had called for, Pauly turned to his lover. "That was fun."

Sloane snuggled against him and whispered, "Blowjobs are always fun."

Pauly snorted out a laugh and kissed Sloane hard and quick on the lips. "I was referring to being on stage together. It's been a long time since we've played such a small venue. I like the intimacy of it, even if we have to sneak out the back afterwards."

"Is that something you'd like to do more of?" Sloane asked.

Pauly slid his arm over the back of Sloane's shoulders, pulling him closer. "Yeah, it is. We make a damn good team."

Sloane was silent for a few minutes. When he looked up at Pauly, his eyes were dancing. "Want to take a road trip?"

"What did you have in mind?"

"How about we make our way across country this week, playing smaller venues until we reach Nashville for New Years?"

"I think that's one of the best ideas I've heard since I suggested we head home to bed." Pauly grinned, pressing his lips against Sloane's.

They were still kissing when the driver said, "Sorry to interrupt, but we're here."

Pauly wasn't embarrassed or sorry. He knew the driver had seen more salacious things in the back seat than two men kissing. "Thank you," he responded before opening his door and holding out his hand for Sloane. After they closed the door behind them, they retrieved their guitars and Sloane's suitcase from the luggage compartment at the back of the SUV. Pauly punched in the code to his gate. He might trust the drivers to keep their whereabouts secret, but he never trusted one of them with the code to get into the property. He could always change the code, but it was a pain in the ass to do so.

Sloane bumped Pauly's shoulder as they walked the short distance to the sidewalk which led to Pauly's front door. "I would say I can't believe you wrote the lyrics to 'The Road Home' at the airport, but you're a musical genius."

Pauly keyed in a different code to unlock the front door, and when it swung open, he pulled Sloane in after him before locking up behind them. After placing the cases on the floor of the foyer, he pulled Sloane to him, wrapping his man in his arms. "I can't believe you played Lenny Kravitz. You know what that song does to me."

"Makes you a sappy mess? Because that's what it always does to me."

Sloane was right. Pauly almost teared up again thinking

57

back to Sloane's performance earlier. Instead of answering, he pulled away, tugging on Sloane's hand, leading him to the bedroom. When they crossed the threshold into the massive room, Pauly stopped in front of Sloane and ran a hand through his lover's long blond hair. "I love your hair loose. Especially when it's hanging down around my face."

"Is that a hint?"

Pauly shook his head. "No, it's an order. You look sexy as fuck tonight, and as much as I love that shirt, I want you naked and riding my cock like you've missed it. Now."

Sloane shivered, and Pauly knew what was about to happen would be different than it had ever been. He made slow work of undressing himself while Sloane tore his own clothes off. When Sloane turned toward the nightstand for lube, Pauly admired Sloane's naked body. Neither one of them were beefy, but Sloane was more toned, and his ass was tight and round. It was one of the reasons Pauly loved taking him from behind. He enjoyed watching his dick sliding in and out of the tight hole while he spanked Sloane's globes until they were bright red.

Not tonight, though. Tonight, he needed to see Sloane's face. It was why he wanted to be ridden. With Sloane straddling Pauly's body, Pauly's hands would be free to touch all that glorious inked skin and have Sloane's jizz covering his chest and stomach when he came.

Sloane handed the lube to Pauly before crawling onto the

bed, presenting his ass to Pauly for prep. Pauly popped the top off the bottle and poured a good bit of the liquid onto his palm. Most of the time, their fucks were quick and dirty with just enough slick so it wouldn't be too painful. Tonight, Pauly wanted slow. He wanted them to make love for the first time since they'd shared their bodies.

Pauly pulled one of Sloane's cheeks back and blew across his pucker before licking a path from his balls up to his hole. He speared his tongue inside, and Sloane pushed back against his face. Normally when Sloane did that it earned him a nice, hard smack, but Pauly wasn't going to make his lover work for it tonight. Replacing his tongue with his slick fingers, he took his time getting Sloane ready, making sure to rub over his prostate several time.

Sloane's moans echoed around the bedroom along with his soft pleas. "Pauly... I need... Please..."

Pauly removed his fingers and placed a kiss on both Sloane's cheeks before crawling onto the bed, settling onto his back. Pauly stroked his cock with his lube-covered fingers and said, "Come here." Sloane didn't hesitate to straddle Pauly's hips, nor did he waste any time sinking down on Pauly's erection. When he bottomed out, Sloane gasped, and Pauly cursed. "Fucking hell, babe. You're so tight." Pauly gripped Sloane's hips when he began moving at a faster pace than Pauly wanted. "Slow down. We have all night to fuck, but right now, I want you to show me how much you love me."

59

Sloane leaned over, resting on his forearms so he could kiss Pauly. His blond hair cascaded around Pauly's face, just like he'd asked. Sloane's tongue danced with Pauly's in the same slow rhythm he moved his hips back and forth. Pauly threaded one hand in Sloane's locks while rubbing the other down his spine and back up. Sloane pulled his mouth away from Pauly's and stared into his eyes. "I think I've loved you forever," he whispered.

Pauly's heart skipped a beat. "I like the sound of forever."

"Yeah?" Sloane's question came out with a grunt.

"Yeah." Pauly cupped both hands on Sloane's face. "God, you're amazing." Pauly had never felt so close to anyone in his thirty-four years. Not even when he'd been with Corinne or Dana, and he'd produced kids with both women. Les Jr. and Juno were products of young hormones and too much alcohol. This was love in its purest form.

Sloane placed his hands on Pauly's chest and said, "I'm not gonna last long. Your dick feels too good."

"Then come for me. I want you to shoot your load all over my chest." Instead of digging his heels into the bed and pumping hard into Sloane's ass like he craved, Pauly continued to let Sloane do the work at the slower pace he needed. He would have his turn being rough later. Pauly slid his fingers over both Sloane's pecs, twisting his nipples, and that was all his lover needed to find his release.

"Pauly... Oh, God..." Sloane's untouched cock pulsed

60

and bobbed as his spunk coated Pauly's stomach and chest. Some managed to reach his chin.

When Sloane's ass tightened around Pauly's dick, he couldn't hold back. Didn't want to hold back. "Fuck. Oh, Slick, fuck." Pauly followed Sloane over the edge, shooting his cum inside Sloane's tight ass. Sloane squeezed his channel, milking Pauly for everything he had.

Sloane reached out a finger and swiped at the cum on Pauly's chin, offering it to Pauly. He sucked Sloane's finger into his mouth, swirling his tongue over the tip. "Mmm, that's better than Mint Chocolate Chip."

Sloane barked out a laugh. "Wow, that's saying something." Pauly was addicted to that particular flavor of ice cream. He'd been known to have Gus pull off the interstate just so Pauly could get his fix.

"Sure is. Why don't you feed me the rest of it?" Pauly propped one arm behind his head and stroked Sloane's side, while Sloane scooped up every drop of jizz and let Pauly lick his fingers clean. When it was all gone, Sloane eased off Pauly's flaccid cock and dropped down next to him on the bed. Pauly wrapped his arm around Sloane and pressed a kiss to his sweaty forehead. "I love you, Slick."

"I love you, too, Les."

***

61

SLOANE REACHED FOR the door handle, but before he could open it, Pauly grabbed his arm and asked, "Are you sure about this?"

They were parked in front of Sloane's garage in Pauly's new Porsche Cayenne. After a night of making love, fucking in the shower, mutual blow jobs, and talking until the early morning, Pauly had taken Sloane with him to the Porsche dealership, where he traded in his Ferrari for an SUV. One of the things they'd discussed while cuddling in bed was spending more time with their kids, and if that happened, they would need more room since they planned on doing so together, starting that morning. Besides that, the SUV was more practical for traveling cross-country with their guitars.

"Sure about us or…?" Sloane held his breath as he waited on Pauly's answer.

"No, babe. Sure about me coming in there," he said, pointing toward the house.

"Of course. We talked about spending time with our kids together."

"Yes, but Tracy and… what's her husband's name?"

"Derik."

"They're in there, too. Isn't that going to be weird?" Pauly was staring out the windshield.

"It's only going to be weird if we stay in the car all morning and don't get out. Come on. There's something I want you to hear." Sloane hadn't shared with Pauly how good

Taryn was on the guitar.

He rounded the hood and waited for Pauly so they could enter his home together. Sloane had already texted Tracy to let her know they were on their way. Before they reached the door, it swung open and Taryn was standing there grinning. "Hi, Uncle Pauly."

"And who might you be?" Pauly asked. Sloane knew he was joking, but the look on Taryn's face was comical.

"It's me, Taryn," she huffed, hands on her hips.

"Can't be. Taryn is just a little slip of a thing, not a half-grown woman." Pauly held his arms open, and Taryn launched herself at him. Even though they'd only met a couple times when the girl was younger, Sloane's daughter was a big fan of all the men in the band. She'd been calling them all 'uncle' since she was old enough to talk. Movement in the doorway had Pauly putting Taryn back on her feet. "Hello, Tracy."

"Pauly. Good to see you again. You're not going to run away this time, I take it?"

Pauly's cheeks flushed, and he shook his head. "No. I'm sorry about yesterday. I had something I needed to take care of."

Tracy didn't look like she believed him, but she didn't call him out. Instead, she moved back and let the three of them come inside. "Pauly, I would like you to meet my husband, Derik. Derik, this is Les Paulson."

63

Derik stepped forward and shook Pauly's hand. "It's nice to meet you." Just like any normal star-struck fan, Derik pumped Pauly's hand longer than necessary. When he realized what he was doing, he pulled away and ducked his head.

"Likewise," Pauly replied, chuckling.

"Come on, Uncle Pauly. There's something I want to show you." Taryn grabbed Pauly's hand and tried to drag him away from her mother. Sloane knew where his daughter was going. Pauly looked back over his shoulder at Sloane.

"You're gonna want to see this," Sloane said, following them to the music room. This time, Tracy and Derik came with them. Sloane entered the room and took the same seat he'd used the day before. When he didn't pick up his guitar, his daughter frowned. "Oh, no. This is all you, kiddo."

Taryn shrugged and placed the strap across her shoulders. Pauly looked at Sloane, raising his eyebrows. Sloane just grinned at his lover when Taryn wasted no time showing them what she'd learned.

Chapter Seven

AN HOUR LATER, after an impromptu jam session with his daughter and his lover, Sloane placed his guitar on the stand and stood, stretching his arms toward the ceiling. He had never been prouder in his life, not even when the band had received their first gold record.

"You keep that up, and you'll be the next Lzzy Hale," Pauly told Taryn.

"Maybe with my playing, but she has a voice that puts everyone to shame. I can't sing worth a crap," Taryn admitted. Sloane wasn't surprised that Taryn knew who the lead singer for Halestorm was.

"Now that your dad and I are off the road, I'd love to spend more time with you, if it's something you're interested in," Pauly offered.

"Seriously?" Taryn looked like she'd just hit the lottery.

"Seriously. He and I already talked about spending more time with our kids, and what better way to spend time with you than honing your craft?"

Taryn stood and threw her arms around Pauly's waist. "Thank you, Uncle Pauly. That would be awesome!"

Holding Taryn in his arms, Pauly looked over her head to Sloane. The look on his face said his best friend felt like he might have won the lottery, too.

Sloane smiled and joined them, pulling Taryn away from Pauly so he could get in on the hugs. "Just keep up your grades, and I promise we'll work with you as much as we can."

"I promise I will, Dad."

Sloane and Pauly joined the others for lunch before he packed his bags for their trip. After promising to see them again soon, he and Pauly climbed into the Porsche and headed out. While Sloane was packing, Pauly had called Echo and told her what they had planned. He asked if she could map out the best small venues for them to play in the next few nights. Most places more than likely had already booked bands since it was the holidays, but being the stars they were, she assured him those bands would love to have the two of them jam with them if not step aside altogether.

Echo hadn't been wrong. All the clubs they stopped at were top notch like Rooster's. They only called the owners or managers right as they were pulling into the town. That way there was less likelihood their appearance would be announced. They weren't trying to be dicks about keeping the fans away; they just wanted to play for the smaller crowds and then get back on the road the next day. All the driving after the late nights was tiring, but it wasn't anything they weren't used to.

They were on their fourth day into their trip, and Sloane was driving. Pauly was tapping away on his cell phone, and when he finally put it down, he said, "Take the next exit."

"What? Where are we going?" Sloane checked the rearview mirror, flipped on the blinker, and maneuvered the Porsche over to the far lane so he could do as Pauly asked.

"I want to ask you something and I don't want you to wreck."

"Okay, now you're scaring me." Sloane took the exit and pulled into a gas station. They needed fuel anyway, so stopping wasn't putting a chink in their drive time.

When they were parked at the pump, Sloane got out and came around to where Pauly was already placing the nozzle in the fuel door. "Pauly, what's going on?"

"I know this isn't the most romantic place to talk about this, but I was thinking." Pauly bit his lip and looked at his shoes.

Okay, now Sloane was really nervous. "About?"

"Were you serious about forever with me?"

"Of course. Pauly, we've been together over half our lives, and we already know everything there is to know about each other. I love you, and yeah, I'm serious."

"Then let's get married."

"What?" Sloane hadn't seen that coming.

"Oklahoma doesn't have a waiting period. We can go to

67

the courthouse, get our marriage license, and be married today."

"You want to marry me?"

"I do. If you'll have me. You're the best part of me, always have been. And I don't want to spend another day without you. Ever."

Sloane grinned at his best friend. "Can you remember the last time we weren't together? You and I have been spent every day with each other for a lot of years."

"And I want to keep that streak alive, only with you as my husband. Let's find a jewelry store and get some rings, and then we'll find the courthouse."

Sloane pulled Pauly to him and kissed him hard. "You're crazy," he said against Pauly's lips when he came up for air. "And I'm crazy about you, so yes. Let's get married."

Clapping and cheering came from the few people who'd also been pumping gas. Pauly smiled and yelled, "He said yes!"

It took over an hour to find a jewelry store that wasn't in a mall, but once they'd found one and purchased rings for each other, they drove to the courthouse, and thirty minutes after walking in, they walked out as husbands.

That night when they called the manager at The Tavern in Oklahoma City, he didn't sound surprised they were in town. When they walked in the back door, they quickly understood why. Echo was standing with the manager, a big grin on her face.

"What are you doing here?" Sloane asked as she launched herself into his arms.

"Celebrating, of course! You didn't invite me to the wedding, but I'm here now."

"How do you know we got married?" Pauly asked.

Echo shook her head. "Well, it's not because you texted me like you promised." Echo smacked Sloane on his arm. "It never ceases to amaze me how the two of you don't check social media. The news of your nuptials hit Twitter five minutes after you left the courthouse. Since The Tavern was on the list of venues I gave you, I hopped the first plane to Oklahoma, and voila! But don't worry, I won't crash your honeymoon night."

The Tavern was packed. Echo had a front row seat, and she wasn't alone. There was a beautiful blonde sitting with their pixie of a manager, and the two of them looked cozy. Maybe it was the bliss running through his soul from being married to Pauly, but he sent out positive vibes into the cosmos that both Echo and Cade would find their own happy ever after.

As with the other nights, he and Pauly switched up the set, mixing older songs with their newer hits. Tossing in a few covers that everyone could sing along with rounded out the night. Echo met them backstage, the blonde standing behind her. "Guys, this is Erin. Erin, Sloane and Pauly."

69

After they shook the woman's hand, Echo said, "Are you headed to Nashville?"

"We are. Thought we might find somewhere quiet to spend New Years together, though, instead of braving downtown. I've heard it's a madhouse down there," Sloane answered. He and Pauly had discussed their plans, and they both agreed on how they wanted to ring in the new year.

"Well, I have it on good authority that Tag's house is empty and waiting for you so you don't have to stay in a hotel," Echo said.

Sloane looked at Pauly, eyebrows raised. "What do you think?"

"I think that's perfect. We'll call him from the road tomorrow and work everything out," Pauly said.

"Excellent. I'm so happy for you both, and I look forward to seeing you soon." Echo pulled the two in for another of her bone-crushing hugs. She took Erin's hand and led the blonde toward the bar.

Pauly pushed Sloane against the wall and whispered in his ear, "What do you say we go consummate this marriage?"

Sloane's cock plumped up, and he pressed it against Pauly's hip. "I say let's go."

After a passion-filled night, Sloane and Pauly made their way down Louisiana, Alabama, and Georgia before heading up to Nashville. They arrived at Tag and Erik's in time for lunch on New Year's Eve. Mack and Bethany, Erik's best friend and office manager, were sitting on the floor playing with Brady and Delilah, while Erik was snapping pictures of the babies.

"Congratulations!" Tag said, pulling them both in for a hug. Erik turned the camera toward them, and they all smiled.

"Thanks," Sloane said.

"And thank you for letting us stay in your house for the next few days," Pauly added.

"It's just sitting there. Since we're living here now, I've decided to put it on the market," Tag said as they walked into the kitchen.

Sloane was planning on selling his house in Malibu once Tracy and Derik had somewhere to go, and Pauly had already spoken to a realtor about his home. He needed to talk to Pauly, but Tag's home would be perfect for them. It had a recording studio as well as plenty of bedrooms if and when their kids decided to come visit.

"I can see the wheels turning, Slick." Pauly smiled and nodded. "Are you thinking it's the perfect place for us?"

"Yeah, I am."

"What? Y'all want to buy my house? You're really planning on staying here in the area?" Tag asked.

"We are. We've talked about our future in the music business, and even if we don't form another band, Nashville is the perfect place for two unemployed musicians." Sloane pulled Pauly to his side and wrapped his arm around his

71

husband's shoulders. Damn, he was still getting used to calling him that. "We've already decided to sell both our houses on the West Coast. This way, we don't have to find a home to remodel to include a studio. Your house already has one. Plus, there's plenty of room for us and our kids when they come visit. Give Gerard a call and have him put the paperwork together."

"Don't you want to know how much the asking price is?" Tag asked.

"Nah. If we can't trust you to give us a good price, who can we trust?" Sloane answered.

Sloane and Pauly spent a couple hours visiting and playing with the babies before they headed to Tag's house. Their house. Tag had given them the keys as well as the code to the gate and alarm. They would decide together what furniture they wanted to have shipped from their own homes and what, if any, of Tag's they would keep. But all that could wait. Even though they'd been married a few days, they were both looking forward to starting their new life together in their new home, and what better time than New Years?

They'd stopped at the store for groceries so they wouldn't have to leave for the next few days if they didn't want. While Pauly was unloading the food, Sloane went upstairs and unpacked their bags, moving Tag's clothes to one of the spare bedrooms, and changed the sheets in the master bedroom. After that was finished, he looked around the room, trying to imagine making it his and Pauly's room.

Strong arms wrapped around him from behind, and Sloane curled his fingers around Pauly's forearms. "I can't believe this is ours. As comfy as that bed looks, I'd really like to put your furniture in here."

"Mine? Why?" Sloane leaned his head back against Pauly's shoulder.

"I've always loved how put together your house is. I hired someone to decorate mine while we were on the road, and it's never felt like home. Just a big, empty, overpriced place to lay my head a couple times a year. Talk about wasteful."

"After we decide what other pieces we want to have shipped, what do you think of having an estate sale and donating the profits?" Sloane asked. He knew where Pauly was coming from. The band had made more money than their great-grandkids would be able to spend, and he had also bought frivolous things just because he could.

"I like that idea. Speaking of ideas, are those fresh sheets?" Pauly pulled Sloane's hair over his shoulder and nuzzled his ear. "Because if they are, I think we should make our own fireworks. It is New Year's Eve, after all."

"Mmm, I like *that* idea."

"Then strip for me." Pauly bit Sloane's lobe and pressed his hard dick against his husband's ass. "Now."

Sloane had always been blessed, but now, with Pauly, he was complete. They had the rest of their lives together, and

73

whether it was playing music on a stage or making love in their bed, they had found their forever in each other.

The End

A Note from the Author

Thank you so much for reading Finding Us. I fell in love with Pauly and Sloane immediately. Their story has been a long time coming, and I'm proud to be part of their happy ever after. If you enjoyed the short story, I would really appreciate a review. One of the best ways you can help an author is to leave a review where you bought the book. It doesn't have to be long, just honest and heartfelt. Another way is suggesting books you love to your friends. Thank you.

Acknowledgments

I usually have a lot of people to thank for helping make my books better than when I finish them. This time, I kept the story close to the vest. Life (most especially trying to write) has been difficult lately with the man having surgery, housetraining a new pup, and the holidays. Thank you to Nikki, Christina, and Candy for your support.

About the Author

Multi-genre author Faith Gibson began writing in high school, and through the years, penned many stories and poems. As her dreams continued getting crazier than the one before, she decided to keep a dream journal. Many of these nighttime escapades have led to a line, a chapter, or even a complete story.

"Love is love, and there's not enough love in the world." This belief she holds strongly, and it's the prevailing theme in her works, all of which come with a happy ending.

Faith believes her purpose in life is to entertain the masses, even if it's one person at a time. Living just outside of Nashville, Tennessee, with the love of her life, when she's not hard at work writing her next adventure, the two of them can often be found playing trivia while enjoying craft beer or off on an adventure of their own.